For Akosua and Naomi

A TEMPLAR BOOK

First published in the UK in 2010 by Templar Publishing
This softback edition published in 2011 by Templar Publishing,
an imprint of The Templar Company Limited,
The Granary, North Street, Dorking, Surrey, RH4 1DN, UK
www.templarco.co.uk

First softback edition

ISBN 978-1-84877-409-4

Edited by Rachel Williams

Printed in China

Ruby Nettleship

and the
Ice Lolly Adventure

Story by Thomas and Helen Docherty
Illustrations by Thomas Docherty

templar publishing

This is **Ruby Nettleship.**

She likes climbing and sliding and running and jumping, and when she isn't doing any of these things, she is dreaming of adventures.

In the park by Ruby's house there was an old, falling-apart
playground. The slide didn't slide, the roundabout
wouldn't go round and the see had lost its saw.

The only thing that worked was the swing, and there was always
a big queue of children waiting to swing on it.

One hot afternoon, Ruby and her friends
had been waiting for ages...

when CRASH!
The swing came un-swung.

Now there was NOTHING to play on and the children
began to wander home.

"Come on, let's go," called Ruby's friends.
But something about the playground made Ruby want to stay.

Without the other children,
the playground felt even sadder
than before.

"No one cares," mumbled Ruby to herself, as she tugged at the broken swing. "If this was my playground there would be loads of brilliant stuff for EVERYONE to play on..."

But just then she was interrupted by the tinkle of an ice cream van. It drew up right next to Ruby.

"Not many people today," remarked
the lady in the van cheerfully.

"The swing broke," explained Ruby.

"Well that won't do," said the lady.
"Here, have an ice lolly."
And she handed Ruby a lolly in a green wrapper.
"It's my last one."

Ruby took the lolly. "Thank you," she remembered to say, but
when she looked up again the ice cream van had vanished.
"That's strange," thought Ruby, turning her attention to the lolly.

It was green like the wrapper, but it seemed to glow from the inside.
She took a bite. It tasted delicious, so she took another one.
The letters 'P' and 'L' appeared on the end of the lolly stick.

Ruby ate the rest of the lolly quickly and held
the stick up to examine it. It read:

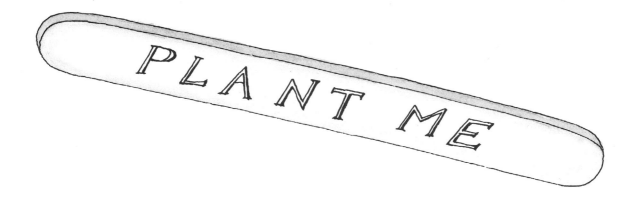

PLANT ME

"I wonder what will happen if I do?" thought Ruby.

No one was about, so she pushed the lolly stick firmly
into the ground, covered it up and waited.

Almost immediately Ruby felt
a rumbling in the ground beneath her.

She watched in amazement
as a multicoloured shoot pushed
its way up through the soil.

It shot up into the air,
nearly hitting her on the nose.

Once it had grown to twice Ruby's
height, it sprouted new branches
that twisted and turned into
a beautiful swing.

"Wow!" cried Ruby.
She climbed aboard
and launched herself into the air.

As Ruby started to swing, more shoots appeared.
They quickly sprouted ladders and poles that blossomed and bloomed
with swings and slides.

Ruby was swinging so high by now that she could see over
the whole city. "I bet no one else is having this much fun,"
she thought to herself.

Then Ruby had an idea.

As if it had read her thoughts, the playground flowered over the whole park and began to spill out into the street.

The first thing Ruby did was to pick up her friends and all the other children who lived nearby.

"This way!" shouted Ruby, and with that, they headed off towards town.

On
the
way,
they
dropped
in
at
the
ZOO...

to see if the animals wanted
to come out and play.

After that, they visited
the supermarket...

and made a GIANT trolley roller coaster.

By the time they got into the centre
of town, the playground was full to bursting.
Even the grown-ups had climbed out of their
cars, put down their shopping, forgotten
about work and joined in the fun.

Soon, the whole city had ground to a halt.

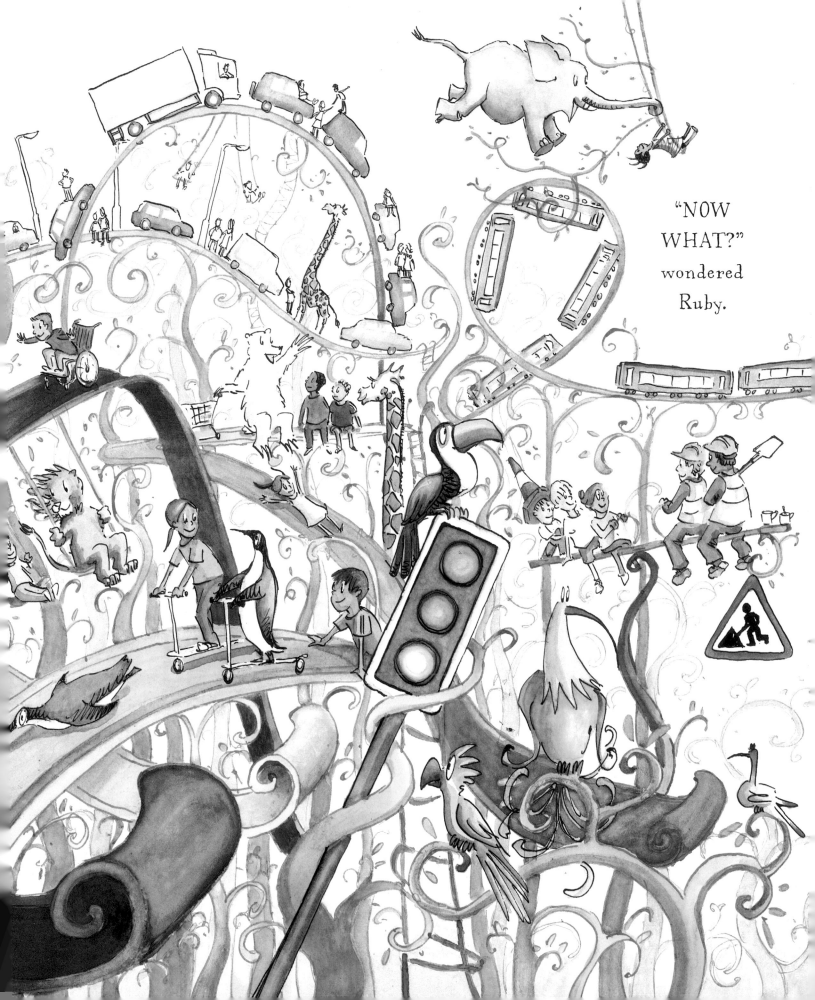

"NOW WHAT?" wondered Ruby.

As if in answer, the playground twisted round and headed
towards a very important-looking building. Before Ruby had
a chance to say anything, she was tipped gently in through
an open window.

Ruby found herself standing in front
of a huge door with THE MAYOR written on it.
"Now I'm in trouble," thought Ruby.
There was nothing else to do, so she took a deep breath and knocked.

"Come in," said a voice that sounded vaguely familiar.

"Ruby Nettleship, I didn't realise that your playground was going to take over the whole city!" remarked the lady sitting behind the desk.

"I'm sorry," said Ruby. "All I wanted was a place for everyone to play, where no one has to wait for the swings."

"I see," replied the lady. "Perhaps you'd better go home for tea and I'll see what I can do."

"Okay," said Ruby, sneaking a quick look out of the window. "Thank you," she remembered to say...

but when she looked back,
the lady behind the desk
had vanished.

Suddenly, Ruby felt
very hungry, so she climbed
out of the window and whispered
one last word to the playground.

As everyone slid home it untangled itself from the city and disappeared back into the ground,

leaving everything just as it had been.

"You're back late," said her mum when Ruby got home.

"Sorry," replied Ruby. "There was a big queue for the swing."

Ruby's dad shook his head. "Someone should do something
about that playground," he said.

Ruby smiled to herself.
"Maybe someone will."